Your Moon, My Moon

A GRANDMOTHER'S WORDS TO A FARAWAY CHILD

PATRICIA MACLACHLAN · ILLUSTRATED BY BRYAN COLLIER

Simon & Schuster Books for Young Readers · New York London Toronto Sydney

SIMON & SCHUSTER BOOKS FOR YOUNG READERS
An imprint of Simon & Schuster Children's Publishing Division
1230 Avenue of the Americas, New York, New York 10020

Book design by Lucy Ruth Cummins
The text for this book is set in Letterpress Text.
The illustrations for this book are rendered in watercolor and collage.
Manufactured in China
0411 SCP
2 4 6 8 10 9 7 5 3 1
Library of Congress Cataloging-in-Publication Data
MacLachlan, Patricia.
Your moon, my moon : a grandmother's words to a faraway child / Patricia MacLachlan ; illustrated by
Bryan Collier.—1st ed.
p. cm.
Summary: Although their homes are different, a grandmother in New England and her loving grandson in
Africa share the same moon.
ISBN 978-1-4169-7950-0 (hardcover : alk. paper)
[1. Grandmothers—Fiction. 2. New England—Fiction. 3. Africa—Fiction.] I. Collier, Bryan, ill.
II. Title
PZ7.M2225Yo 2010
[E]—dc22
2008050451
ISBN 978-1-4169-8261-6 (eBook)

With love, for my granddaughter, Ella Nuru MacLachlan—
born July 22, 2006, Dar es Salaam, Tanzania

—P. M.

With all the world's problems, separations, and distractions,
I dedicate this book to every child and adult who misses someone they love.
The moon has always been there, serving as a point of reference for all of us to connect.
Thank God for the moon.

—B. C.

A snowflake falls

where I live.

Then another.

Silent,

soft,

light as your breath.

One,

two,

three.

The sun is hot

where you live.

So far away.

Fire finches fly up in the trees

hoping for shade.

You can count them.

Four,

five,

six.

When you were little, I visited you and we read books.

All the books,

one after the other after the other.

You loved the freight train book

even though you had never seen one in your life.

Tr

Now you like every single book about the moon—
you love the moon.

There is ice on the pond where I live.

Slippery,

shiny,

slick.

If you were here, I would hold your hand

and skate with you

across the pond.

The wind swirling wisps of snow

around us.

You would laugh.

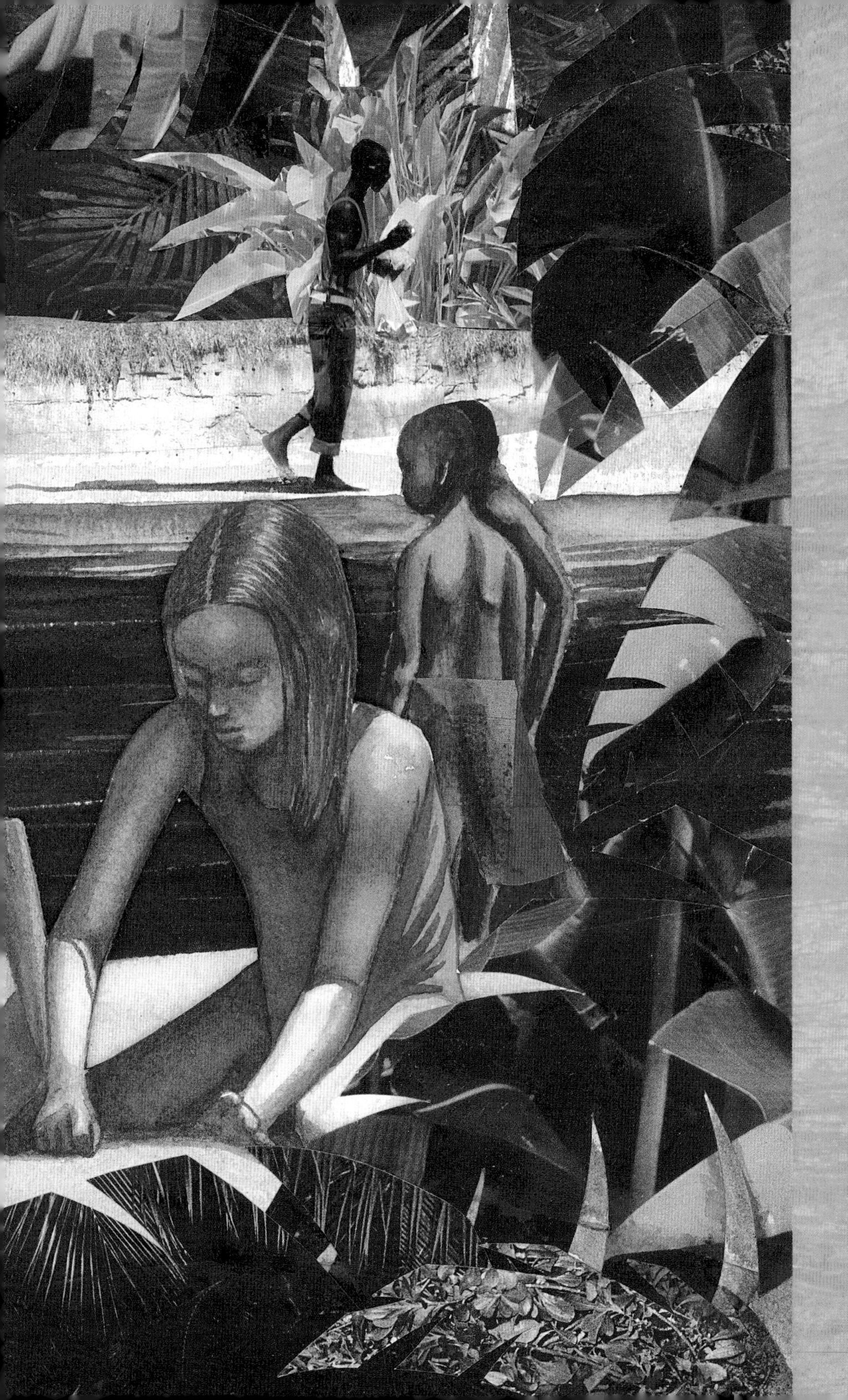

If I were where you live,

we would swim in the gleaming lake

where the fish eagle flies.

We would build castles in the white sand

and watch the monkey babies

on their mother's backs.

Maybe one would steal your banana.

I would laugh.

Where you live the dogs love you—

Bossi and Wups,

who want the food you drop,

and big old Tanga with the sweet face,

who lets you lean against him

and comb his hair

and kiss him.

He protects you from all things.

When you came to see me,

my dogs loved you too.

They followed you everywhere you went.

Now when they walk up my mountain road,

their noses to the ground,

they look for grouse

and rabbits

and deer.

Mostly, they look for you

because they miss you.

In the morning where I live

the sun rises above the mountains,

a shining

red

ball

that changes to yellow as I watch.

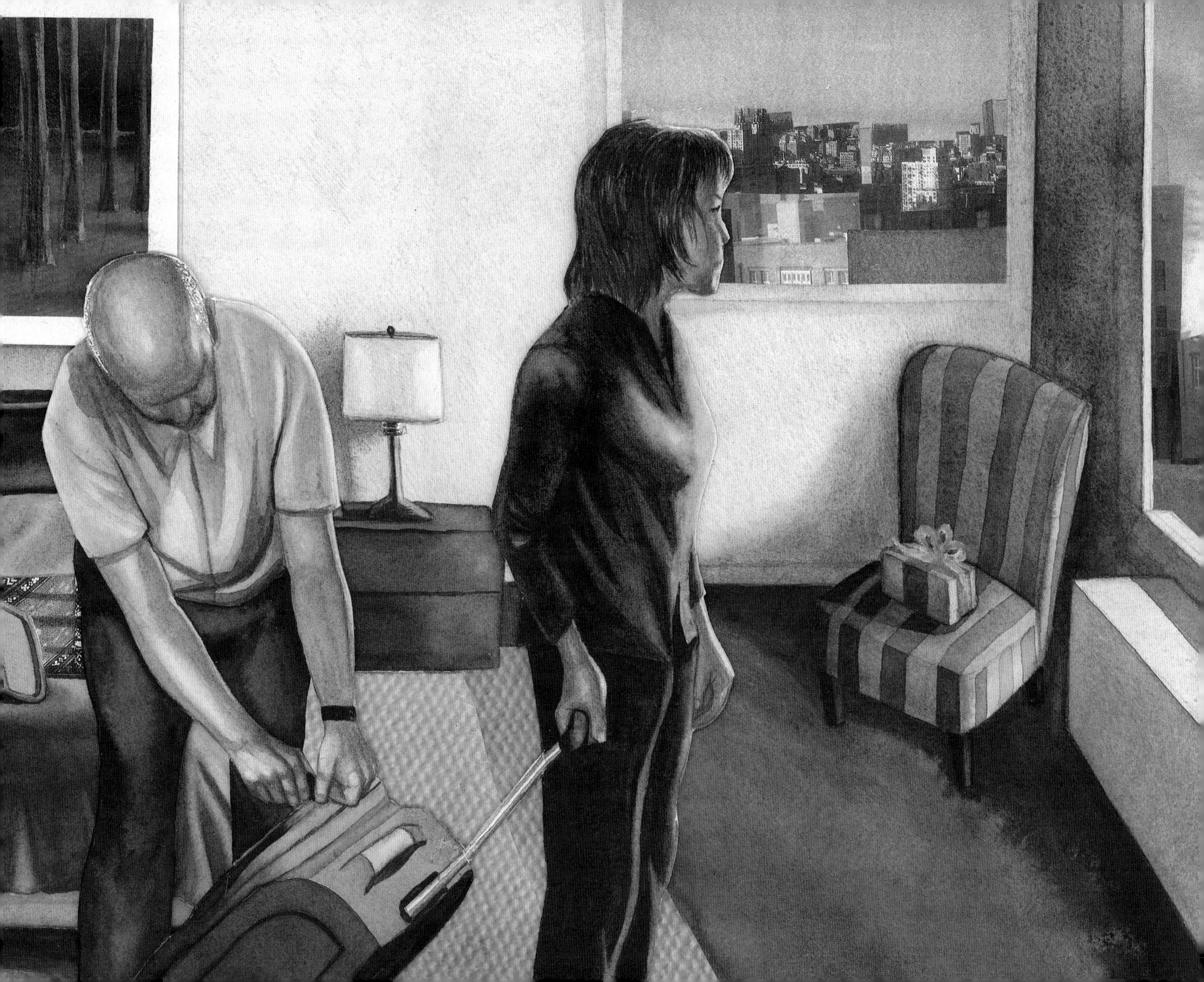

On your hilltop

above the lake,

the sun drops at night

and paints the sky and water

and the dogs and your mama

and papa

red and pink and orange.

And then you see your moon.

Where I live we sleep under

quilts

and wear woolly socks

when it is cold.

When I sleep, I dream about you:

how you laugh when your mama sings,

how you like to walk everywhere in your

rubber boots,

how you check the chicken house for eggs—

Broody is your favorite hen.

Where you live you sleep under a netting
like a royal child,
safe from buzzing mosquitoes.
Do you dream about me?
Walking with my dogs?
Do you remember the books I read you, the words
falling around us both like a blanket?
Do you hear the songs I sang you when you were
a baby?

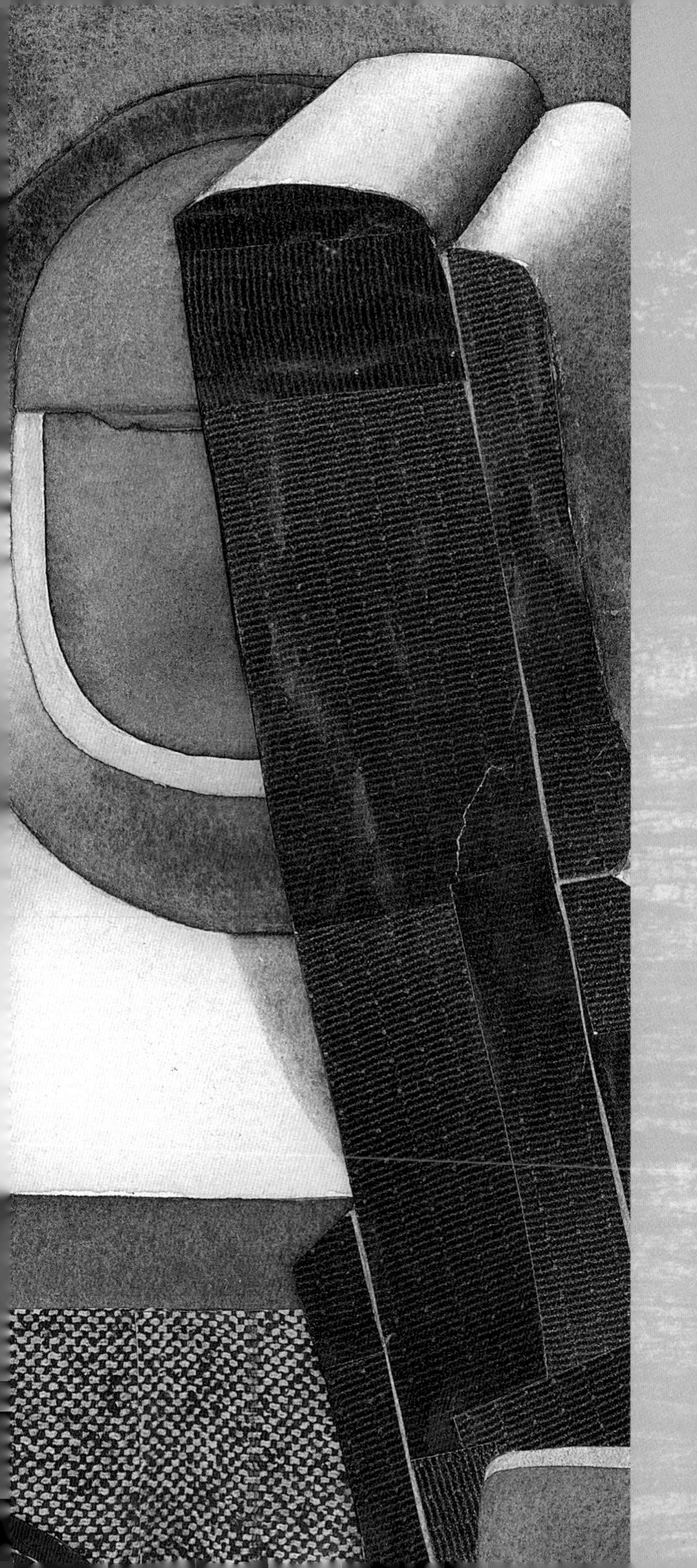

I sing the songs I sang to you every night.

I sing them

so I will remember you,

hoping that you will remember me too,

even though I am here

and you are there.

Every night you look for your moon.

Every night I look for mine.

Your moon is my moon too.